The Bard of Withering Heights

Nostalgic truths, observations, and wisecracks about life in small-town America

Words by Tom Cordell
Pictures by Bernie Kapuza

The Bard of Withering Heights: Nostalgic truths, observations, and wisecracks about life in small-town America

Copyright © 2018 Tom Cordell. All rights reserved. No part of this book may be reproduced or retransmitted in any form or by any means without the written permission of the publisher.

Published by Wheatmark®
2030 East Speedway Boulevard, Suite 106
Tucson, Arizona 85719 USA
www.wheatmark.com

ISBN: 978-1-62787-607-0 (paperback)
ISBN: 978-1-62787-608-7(ebook)
LCCN: 2018937029

A Bit About The Bard

The Bard is a mischievous observer and commentator on all aspects of life in Withering Heights, a slice of small-town America. Inspired by great American humorists like country philosopher Frank McKinney "Kin" Hubbard and Tom K. Ryan, creator of Tumbleweeds, the Bard delights in uncovering amusing truths in human nature, where most people try to hide them.

Scorning political correctness and strictly avoiding work, the Bard prefers musing and mingling with the prominent citizens of Withering Heights, some of whom you will meet very soon. They have a lot to say about life, love, and many other aspects of human experience. Impish and unrepentant, the Bard and his friends are delightful company for a few moments or a full evening. Come in and get to know them!

Meet the Celebrated Citizens of Withering Heights

The Bard	Narrator, truth seeker, and resident philosopher
Princess Merry Babbler	Stylish and uber-talkative teenager
Jake Clover	Old-school everyman
Darla Chiffon	Effervescent aging prom queen
Aunt Birdie Babbler	Insatiable gossipmonger and busybody
Renaldo Breeze	Devastatingly handsome and charming ladies' man
Bea Babbler	Matriarchal family sage and book lover
Boomer Bailey	Used-car salesman and securities hustler
Brother Bob Babbler	Steadfast junior high teacher, father, and barbecue guru
Reverend Ray Bob Dooley	Evangelical preacher and internet religion blogger
Withering Heights Furballs	Dogs and their well-trained human companions
Roxanne Clover	Former roller derby queen and wife of Jake
Grandpa Bud Babbler	Cantankerous and stubborn senior citizen
Arlo Berry	Woeful and beleaguered husband
Ernestine Grizzle	Irascible school librarian
Sue Ellen Springer	Frequently married former cheerleader

Maxine Mooney	Frequently widowed hot-tempered activist and mega-gardener
Trip and Buffy Barnswallow	Stylish but dim social climbers
Pooh Gauzy McFaddish	Snobbishly clueless society columnist
Winslow "TAC" Hammer	Celebrity judge and golf instructor
Carlyle Puffington	Fat cat banker and real estate tycoon
Hilda Bunswaggle	Overdramatic amateur actress
Dudley Clover	Son of Jake and not much else. Not the brightest light on the scoreboard
Leonard "Bytes" Dupree	Computer programmer and part-time bookie
Frosty LaRue	Entrepreneurial theater owner and choreographer
J. Wadsworth Fifeington	Pompous and privileged heir to a septic tank fortune
Newt Buckley	Paroled political fundraiser and tax assessor
Bartley Twittle	Perpetual college student and work-avoidance specialist
Earl Dingo	Divorced auto mechanic
Slats Bombauer	Journalist for the *Withering Heights Tattler*

The Bard Welcomes You to Withering Heights!

Like Camelot, Avalon, or Neverland, Withering Heights is an idyllic spot nestled between fantasy and reality. It is a timeless place that reflects life in small-town America, past and present... a collection of thoughts and feelings, wit and wisdom, and enduring ideas that spring from human experience. The citizens of Withering Heights confirm that human nature doesn't change despite the fast-paced modern world that swirls around us. People are the same as they've always been – male and female, young and old, married and single, pleasant, eccentric, maddening, funny, irascible, friendly, contradictory, unique, imperfect, and very, very human. As the resident narrator of life in Withering Heights, it is my pleasure to bring to light the characters who inhabit our little town... characters who are very likely to appear wherever you live as well. Their thoughts and actions reveal many humorous and sometimes uncomfortable truths of human nature, especially those truths that people hate to admit. Come in and take a stroll around Withering Heights. You'll find things to laugh about and think about, and you might just recognize someone you know!

Musings from the Bard

❝ One thing marriage teaches you is that being right is overrated.

People who don't have any fun always want to pass a law against it.

Between the mess in Washington, the mood of the people, and gladiator shoes for women, the nation has just about reached its limit of ugliness.

Even a woman with a model husband wants to change him into a different model.

Never irritate the cook or the bookkeeper.

It's a wonder that a fool and his money ever get together in the first place. ❞

❝ It's hard to appreciate gangsta rap music at any volume louder than 'mute.'

We would rather take a calculus test on a roller coaster than try to sort out the everyday dramas of teenagers.

'All things being equal' is a pretty good motto for a plastic surgeon.

Reverend Ray Bob Dooley was out at his uncle's sheep farm yesterday trying out his new sermon.

People love to see the mighty fall, but it's even more fun to watch the pompous and the pious get what's coming to them.

Nobody ever got married just to test the idea of sharing a bathroom. ❞

" Never debate gun control with an armed robber.

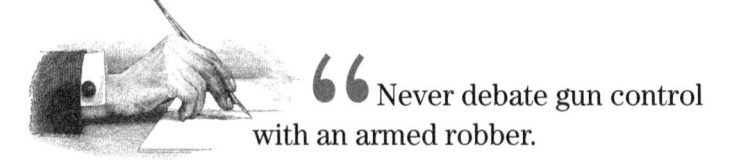

There is no pacifying a woman who is unhappy with her hair.

Whenever men talk about sex or money, there is at least one liar in the conversation.

Hardly anything is more annoying than being a good sport.

Live and let live works until somebody owes you money.

Nobody ever complains about the cost of true love or ice cream. "

Princess Merry Babbler

An ultrahip teenager, the Princess is the quintessential social butterfly. A social-media fanatic, her total number of online followers is just slightly less than the population of the Western Hemisphere.

The Princess also holds the world record for the most cell phone minutes ever used by any human being or small business in a single month. A budding business executive, she excels at handling money – especially her parents'. Described by her mother, Bea Babbler, as "my hundred-miles-per-hour child," the Princess is also a tireless shopper whose first word as a baby was "VISA." Since she started driving, the Princess has worn out eight tires, two sets of brakes, three fenders, and both of her parents. Mailboxes are in mortal danger whenever she backs out of a driveway.

> Princess Merry Babbler now has an outfit for every occasion except cleaning her room.

Princess Merry Babbler's boyfriend is learning French, which makes him unsuitable in two languages.

Princess Merry Babbler is only shopping until six o'clock during Lent.

Princess Merry Babbler has a fondness for mirrors, especially when they are attached to a car.

You could explain algebra to an antelope before you could convince Princess Merry Babbler that silence is golden.

Princess Merry Babbler spent all day at the mall and finally found something she didn't want.

❝ Ladies' man Renaldo Breeze is quite a philosopher. He says, 'Women truly resemble art. Both are uniquely beautiful, and both are greatly diminished by any attempt to understand them completely.'

Jake Clover blows cigar smoke like he's trying to inflate a pool toy.

When Newt Buckley reads a newspaper, he looks like he's hiding from the law.

Sue Ellen Springer repeated her wedding vows at the courthouse today while renewing her marriage to her cell phone.

Boomer Bailey and his brother-in-law went shopping together and bought their wives the same dress for Christmas. Both divorces are pending.

Women love any compromise that includes going out to dinner. ❞

> In raising children, the terrible twos are nothing compared to the terrible tattoos.

A woman who is smart, rich, and beautiful is more than most men can get... and more than most women can stand.

Everyone who is married secretly thinks they live with the world's worst driver.

Earl Dingo's nephew never goes hunting because of his uncanny resemblance to a moose.

One of the most annoying people anywhere is the fellow who always finds a parking place.

A word to the unwise is never enough.

Jake Clover

An old-school regular guy and bar-napkin artist, Jake is a somewhat reliable source of information about anything in Withering Heights that isn't too complicated. Married to a former roller derby queen, Jake is an adequate plumber, a mediocre Little League coach, and a TV remote expert who can identify seventeen brands of beer nuts while blindfolded.

An all-seasons sports fan, he likes to reminisce about his glory days playing class D baseball for the Withering Heights Wombats. Today, Jake is an accomplished procrastinator and cigar smoker who hasn't been in a gym since the Reagan administration.

Jake says his bad habits look much worse when he sees them in someone else. All in all, the common man doesn't get any more common than Jake.

" Jake Clover finally started a savings plan today with six quarts of whiskey.

Jake Clover says he hangs around the bar after the ball game because 'if I go home, they'll hand me a rake.'

Jake Clover says he hates to sit in the corner of a room because it reminds him of being in school.

'It isn't good to think too much about dying, unless you're at the opera,' says Jake Clover.

A team of archeologists has received a grant to dig their way through Jake Clover's garage.

Jake Clover says he doesn't exercise because he hates to get cigar ashes on his jogging suit. "

“Well, it's the thought that counts,” said Maxine Mooney, after missing her husband with all six shots.

Judge Winslow 'TAC' Hammer bangs his gavel like he is dispensing walnuts instead of justice.

Hardly anybody makes a long story short enough.

There just doesn't seem to be any way to separate loud and stupid.

Figures don't lie, which explains the popularity of fitness centers.

No computer on earth has more memory than a woman recalling a love affair.

“ Southern California has lots of beautiful old cars and high-society women, but not many of them have their original equipment.

Women are just naturally against spitting, even in the home.

Any man who is blunt and brutally honest will always be admired by his fellow bachelors.

By popular demand, the Tuesday special at Big Wanda's Café is no meatloaf.

Some husbands think it is easier to pay alimony than to pick up a wet bath towel.

Everything heals faster when you're young, including a broken heart. ”

Darla Chiffon

A beloved former Withering Heights prom queen, Darla is now a radio talk-show host, a decorated hair and makeup artist, and a successful beauty pageant operator. Winner of America's Biggest Hair competition from 2005 to 2007, Darla puts plenty of perky into everything she does.

A trendy home decorator who recently remarried (again), Darla is now busy remodeling her kitchen and her new husband. Darla is also a legendary cosmetologist, whose sold-out beauty seminars show young girls how to put on makeup without using a trowel. Her Miss Charming and Delightful beauty pageant is an annual extravaganza, and her weekly radio show, *How to Look Better than Usual,* is a Withering Heights favorite.

❝ Darla Chiffon just bought a new red convertible with plenty of room for her hair.

Darla Chiffon has added her new husband to her list of things around the house that don't work.

Darla Chiffon is always trying to do something with her hair – like keep her husband out of it.

Darla Chiffon says, 'No matter how many new beauty treatments they come up with, there is always a new wrinkle.'

Darla Chiffon is no artist, but her clothes can draw a crowd. ❞

❞ Society columnist Pooh Gauzy McFaddish isn't afraid to take on the tough social issues. Lately she has been leading the fight for new butter molds at the country club.

We'll say this for baby boomers – most of us don't wear lodge hats.

Men think they don't understand women, but women think men don't understand anything.

Two ignoramuses never argue quietly.

After two weeks of dieting, amateur actress Hilda Bunswaggle has lost a considerable amount of congeniality.

Common knowledge is most common in a small town. ❞

"'Some people are made miserable by circumstances, while others just have a natural talent for it,' says Brother Bob Babbler.

Not even a fool and his money get parted sooner than the back of a hospital gown.

If you want peace and quiet on an airplane, just ask the person next to you if they've been saved.

A new study shows that two major causes of deafness are loud music and getting elected.

Other than a supermodel moving in next door, the most unlikely thing is a bride who doesn't think her new husband needs a few changes.

Voters pay the price for ignorance when Congress gets in session."

Aunt Birdie

Aunt Birdie is a gossip goddess who has never heard a rumor she didn't repeat. Birdie is the lifetime president of the Tongues of Fire Hearsay Society of Withering Heights, whose motto is, "You heard it here first."

A free-spirited adventurer, Aunt Birdie also leads Wayne Newton groupies on an annual motorcycle trip to Branson, Missouri.

Birdie loves gossip and gardening because they both involve digging up dirt. Beloved by neighborhood children because she trades candy for information, Birdie claims she can gather a week's worth of juicy rumors with one bag of red licorice.

Her husband is mostly deaf – by choice.

❝ 'Well, damn, that's a first,' said Aunt Birdie Babbler's husband when she told him she bit her tongue.

Aunt Birdie Babbler kept a secret for forty-three minutes today, achieving a personal best.

Aunt Birdie Babbler's recent spring garden party displayed a colorful variety of rumors.

Gossip queen Aunt Birdie Babbler loves peanut butter, but it doesn't keep her tongue from slipping.

'While cleaning up for company, I always set aside a little dirt for conversation,' says Aunt Birdie Babbler.

Gossip queen Aunt Birdie Babbler says summer wine makes a dandy truth serum. ❞

❝ The Full Swanky Women's Club of Withering Heights has canceled the rest of its spring cotillion classes after the food fight at last night's dance.

FULL SWANKY Women's Club

Maxine Mooney was missing her ex-husband today, so she went out and bought a pet snake.

To err is human... to forgive is not likely.

Young Bartley Twittle is such a good golfer that he's thinking about becoming an insurance agent.

The only thing more transparent than a clean window is a false compliment.

Hardly anybody remembers how to forgive and forget. ❞

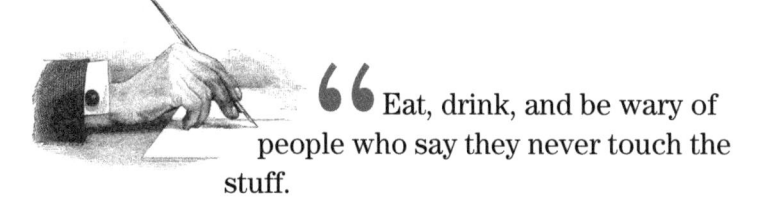

" Eat, drink, and be wary of people who say they never touch the stuff.

Popularity breeds much more contempt than familiarity.

News travels fast when it's men telling lies or women telling secrets.

In politics, it seems like the smallest minds always have the biggest mouths.

Trendy society couple Trip and Buffy Barnswallow are getting divorced this weekend, having exhausted all other ideas for a holiday party.

Even when you're out of work, you still keep earning your reputation. "

Renaldo Breeze

A devastatingly handsome bachelor, advertising executive, and art film producer, Renaldo oozes charm as the ultimate ladies' man. Dynamic and supremely confident, Renaldo overpowers a room when he walks in – and that's just his cologne. A poet and philosopher who fervently studies the fairer sex, he says most men strike out with women because they talk to the ladies like they are ordering a new water heater. A gourmet cook and former underwear model, Renaldo is now developing an internet course on the fine art of winking. His best-selling book, *One Hundred Pickup Lines for Clueless Guys*, is available at every bar in Withering Heights.

❝Charming bachelor Renaldo Breeze offers this advice: 'To make the ladies swoon, just act like a bad boy who is trying to reform.'

Successful ladies' man Renaldo Breeze says one sure way to fascinate a woman is to sit and really listen to her.

Gourmet bachelor Renaldo Breeze says he loves grocery stores because they are full of food and women.

Renaldo Breeze swears that his only bad habit is being cheerful in the morning.

Stylish bachelor Renaldo Breeze always knows the latest ways to attract the ladies. Lately, he's been standing pretty far away from his razor.

Renaldo Breeze advises, 'Forget about flowers and candy. To really impress a woman, tell her you would love to help her remodel her bathroom.'❞

❝ You could put ballet slippers on a warthog before you could win a political argument on Facebook.

If we can't have peace, can we at least try for quiet?

J. Wadsworth Fifeington, pompous heir who likes to brag that his family came over on the Mayflower, says he has the parole records from England to prove it.

The search for general agreement on anything continues.

Bartley Twittle, who is still too young to marry for money, is considering light employment.

Nothing is harder to take than good advice from an unemployed relative. ❞

"Society columnist Pooh Gauzy McFaddish says the Full Swanky Women's Club of Withering Heights has just donated 250 finger bowls to help the homeless.

One thing that money can definitely buy is more expensive mistakes.

There is nothing idle about gossip once a small town gets a hold of it.

Two things that will always divide men and women are devotion to sports and hair.

Aunt Birdie Babbler is confined to home after the dog ate her false teeth.

Next to a big breakfast of sausage, eggs, and pancakes, nothing sticks with you like a high school nickname."

Bea Babbler

The Babbler family sage, Bea is a dog lover and voracious reader who hosts the annual Book Babes Beach Bash each summer. A fabulous baker, she believes dark chocolate is pure love in an edible form.

Bea is also an up-to-the-minute news junkie and MENSA member who has never lost a political argument – or any other kind. She is highly skilled at spotting phonies and spoiling grandchildren, and she can almost tolerate Republicans at a safe distance.

A proud liberal, Bea says the only problem with being a Democrat is that you can't really enjoy owning anything that's better than average.

Bea is adored by her family and her husband, who lives to serve the queen.

❝ Bea Babbler sprained her nose today while walking past a chocolate factory.

Bea Babbler says a dandy birthday present for a teenage daughter is some pearls of wisdom.

Bea Babbler has a busy day today. She has to get her hair done before she meets with a woman she doesn't like.

Bea Babbler just installed a GPS in her dryer to find lost socks.

Bea Babbler is tired of hearing about women being bad drivers. What's more, she thinks men should have to get a special permit to operate a grocery cart.

'Marriage is one of the few things that can grow stronger as it grows old,' says Bea Babbler. ❞

❝ Sue Ellen Springer says the best husbands are like the best furniture – comfortable, versatile, and worth some money.

Ladies' man Renaldo Breeze observes, 'It seems like everything most men know about women came from a junior high locker room.'

'I think a country that can build supercomputers and space shuttles ought to be able to make a sliding screen door that stays on the track,' says Grandpa Bud Babbler.

Jake Clover says his brother-in-law is a jack of all trades and a doer of none.

Other than a neighbor who decorates his yard with pink plastic flamingos, no visitor is less welcome than some telltale sign of getting older.

We wonder why people who tape their glasses together can't see what they look like. ❞

❝ Jake Clover says the best way to fix brussels sprouts is to burn the crop.

We wish Saint Patrick was still around to drive the snakes out of Washington.

Auto mechanic Earl Dingo is due for an oil change on his hair.

No parents ever wore out a camera on their third child.

Slats Bombauer says he became a journalist because he likes working nights and he's too noisy to be a thief.

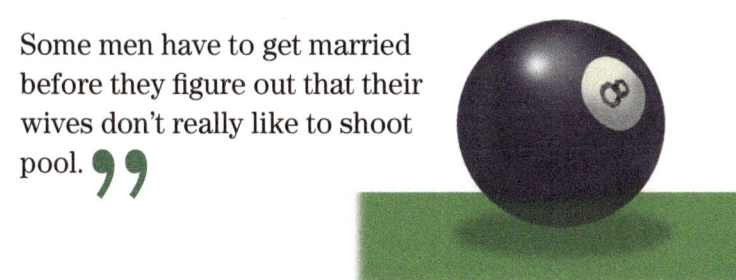

Some men have to get married before they figure out that their wives don't really like to shoot pool. ❞

Boomer Bailey

An irresistible used-car salesman and part-time penny stockbroker, Boomer has not told the whole truth about anything since 1979. Descended from a long line of con men, Boomer's great-grandfather made a fortune selling snake oil off the back of a wagon. To close a deal, Boomer once promised a free lunch at the Withering Heights Sushi Palace with his close personal friend Lady Gaga.

A congenial liar who is quick with a joke, Boomer is lots of fun to have around as long as nobody is doing any business. He's a clothes horse who dresses on the wild side, and all of Boomer's ties look like he lost a bet.

His collection of white shoes and white belts is second to none in Withering Heights.

"Jake Clover went down to Boomer's Auto World and told Boomer Bailey he'd like to see a good used car. 'By God, so would I,' said Boomer.

Used-car salesman Boomer Bailey got up late today and accidentally picked a shirt and tie that matched.

When Boomer Bailey eats soup, he looks like he's bailing out a rowboat.

After years of selling cars in a cold climate, Boomer Bailey wants to move to Florida so he can lie in the sun.

Jake Clover says the only thing that comes around slower than springtime in Withering Heights is Boomer Bailey's turn to buy lunch."

❝ You could paddle a canoe in a cornfield before you would ever see somebody pick a paint color on the first try.

The things you aren't supposed to know about somebody are always the most fun.

Next to a grouch with a toothache, nothing is harder to take care of than a friendship based on money.

There is no hope for someone who tries to relieve frustration by playing golf.

Next to a daughter's boyfriend, the hardest thing to dislodge is a political opinion.

We've just about run out of social occasions that will make anyone shave. ❞

❝ Men's Guide to Home Decorating, Rule #37: A vase is a 'vahhhze' when it costs more than one hundred dollars.

Some teenage girls use cosmetics like they are trying to make up a whole new identity.

Hardly anything is more fun than eating spaghetti while wearing an old shirt.

There is always a silver lining. For instance, a marriage of two orphans is a dandy solution to in-law problems.

Aside from an amateur opera, nothing lasts longer than a bad reputation.

Fat cat banker Carlyle Puffington won't tell his age, but he's old enough to wear argyle socks. ❞

Brother Bob Babbler

A fearless and unflappable junior high school teacher and RV driver who can park anywhere, Brother Bob is now maneuvering through the early stages of fatherhood and husband training.

He has already discovered that one of the hardest things in marriage is translating what's being said into what it really means. Brother Bob is a barbecue rib connoisseur and budding grill master who developed his own secret sauce in his school's chemistry lab.

A lifelong fan of the Withering Heights Wombats baseball team, he has an autographed picture of Jake Clover.

According to his mother, Bea Babbler, Brother Bob and his wife are doing a wonderful job of raising the cutest children on earth.

" Brother Bob Babbler says, aside from an expectant father, no one is more anxious than a dog sitting by a barbecue.

'Endurance is a quality to be greatly admired in athletes and junior high school teachers,' says Brother Bob Babbler.

According to Brother Bob Babbler, the best way to enjoy a big family picnic is to keep your ears open and your mouth full of potato salad.

Brother Bob Babbler says taking a vacation with children is like taking a nap at a heavy metal concert.

Young husband Brother Bob Babbler doesn't know who created the unwritten laws of marriage, but he's learning who enforces them.

Brother Bob Babbler says his friend who is quitting school to get married is putting the heart before the course. "

" After raising three teenage daughters, Carlyle Puffington has quit banking to become a drama teacher.

After giving it a two-hour nap test, Jake Clover says his new TV chair is going to work out just fine.

Any parent with teenage children will never be scared of pickpockets.

It's hard to imagine that even a civilized society needs more than two polo teams.

The more popular something is today, the funnier it will look in ten years.

Hunting season is almost over, and Jake Clover still can't find his glasses. "

❝ Recent divorcé Earl Dingo says, 'I don't think much of the women in singles' ads. They all want to dance.'

It must be enjoyable to be an undertaker and not have to chitchat with your customers.

Of all the things we don't see anymore, we miss the neighborhood ice cream truck the most.

Actions speak louder than anything except TV commercials.

It's funny to hear about an actor making a comeback when we've never heard of him in the first place.

A wise man appreciates any woman who winks at life— or at him. **❞**

Reverend Ray Bob Dooley

Like his good friend Darla Chiffon, Reverend Ray Bob Dooley is a homegrown media star who began life in Withering Heights as Freddy Funkwhistle. Starstruck at an early age, Freddy headed out to Hollywood to become a sitcom writer. After three years of life in the fast lane, he staggered into a Palm Springs rehab center. It was there Freddy found religion and social media, emerging after six weeks as Reverend Ray Bob Dooley, Internet Evangelist to the Stars!

After getting his online seminary degree in video production, Reverend Ray Bob set up shop back home in Withering Heights. An instant success, his pay-as-you-pray blog delivers inspirational sermons on how to keep the Lord in your life for only $9.95 per week. A shrewd businessman who worships the holy profits, Reverend Ray Bob also sells genuine religious relics on his website when he has time to make them.

❝ Reverend Ray Bob Dooley's new suit is louder than a quarter hitting the church collection plate.

'The cost of sin is as high as ever, but it is still a best seller,' observes Reverend Ray Bob Dooley.

Reverend Ray Bob Dooley's new sixty-dollar haircut certainly looks the part.

Reverend Ray Bob Dooley advises, 'An occasional trip to hell, while never pleasant, is always instructive.'

Reverend Ray Bob Dooley is offering an internet special this month on prayers for receding hairlines. ❞

❝ 'Whoever said women are the fair sex never argued with one,' says Jake Clover.

Former cheerleader Sue Ellen Springer is still plenty active, having just jumped into her fourth marriage.

Dudley Clover won't eat navel oranges because he wants to join the army.

Some people need a lot more improvement that just getting older and wiser.

No one is more irritating than the fellow who knows slightly more than nothing about everything.

Most of the time, the best thing to say is not much. ❞

❝ Darla Chiffon and her cat have decided her new husband is mostly trainable.

Nobody talks more with less effect than a backseat driver.

Thanks to the internet, it is now possible to simultaneously waste time with people all over the world.

The only people who will tell you the absolute truth are a child and a drunk.

Princess Merry Babbler is at home recovering from a recent disruption of cell phone service.

A bore is someone more likely to be struck by lightning than by an interesting thought. ❞

Withering Heights Furballs

A loyal and dependable friend is one of life's great joys...especially when that friend is a dog.

Just like the quirky people they live with, the dogs of Withering Heights come in all sizes, shapes, and personalities. Jake and Roxanne Clover share their life with Sluggo, a slobbering hulk of a bulldog who, like Jake, doesn't move much until it's time for dinner.

Meanwhile, Bea Babbler has a flat-coated retriever named Edison who is bright, full of energy, and eager to try any new idea.

Princess Merry Babbler adores her little Gucci Poochie, a shih tzu who loves mirrors and going to the pet store to check out the latest dog fashions.

Roameo, a handsome blue-eyed rascal who belongs to Renaldo Breeze, enjoys wandering around town from yard to yard and visiting the ladies.

One of Roameo's favorites is Chanel, Darla Chiffon's high-society Afghan hound, who never lifts a paw for anyone unless they are doing her nails.

Across town, Reverend Ray Bob Dooley's border collie, Moses, is always busy helping the reverend shepherd and fleece his flock.

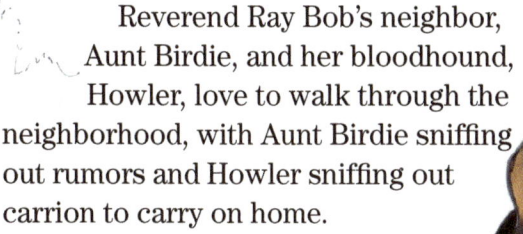

Reverend Ray Bob's neighbor, Aunt Birdie, and her bloodhound, Howler, love to walk through the neighborhood, with Aunt Birdie sniffing out rumors and Howler sniffing out carrion to carry on home.

Every day is dog day in Withering Heights!

❝ A sense of humor doesn't fit some people any better than a Mexican sombrero.

Tax assessor Newt Buckley says two things that always disagree with him are tomatoes and the general public.

No one ever has faith in someone else's idea of God.

We should be running from a lot of people who are running for office.

After six years of high school, Dudley Clover was just named Most Likely to Be Easily Amused.

Of all the mysteries that have baffled mankind for centuries, the most intriguing is wondering what really lies behind a woman's smile. ❞

" Jake Clover has given up on getting rich. Now he just hopes his epitaph reads Paid in Full.

A lot of people let their chance of a lifetime slip by once they find out how much work is involved.

Speaking of ideal physical attributes, two of the very best are being open-minded and close-mouthed.

Leonard 'Bytes' Dupree, who left home last Tuesday in search of a good used computer, remains at large.

Speaking of things that made a clean getaway, whatever happened to good manners?

There is a good reason why tofu doesn't look good enough to eat. "

Roxanne Clover

Born into a sports-loving family, Roxanne is the daughter of "Mad Dog" Martinez, a Withering Heights football legend who once broke a wooden goalpost with his helmet while scoring a game-winning touchdown. Described by her father as "a good girl, strong like bull," Roxanne was banned from her high school football team only because she beat up too many of the boys during practice.

Later, while training to become a professional mud wrestler, Roxanne discovered roller derby. She quickly became "Rockin' Roxie," a star attacker for the Withering Heights Blasters. One night during a match, it was love at first sight when she got knocked over the rink wall and landed in Jake Clover's lap. Jake says Roxanne has a big heart and is always bringing home strays, which is how she got Jake. Married to Jake for twenty-two years, Roxanne says, "I love him, but sometimes he drives me crazy. Between Jake and my car, it's a tossup as to which one is harder to start in the morning."

❝Roxanne Clover, who sang 'Stand by Your Man' to a packed house at the Karaoke Klub last night, has given up betting with her husband.

Roxanne Clover says she never cared much about history until she went to Jake's high school reunion.

Roxanne Clover just became the first woman to win the shin-kicking contest at the Fourth of July picnic.

Roxanne Clover says she never cusses, except every day at her husband.

Roxanne Clover is very handy around the house. Her husband, Jake, says it's like being married to Bob Vila without the beard.❞

❝ Jake Clover says, 'For some reason, my wife believes I can do what I'm doing plus what she wants me to do all at the same time.'

The internet makes it possible to find enough information to support any bad idea.

Bea Babbler wants her husband to have a rummage sale to get rid of his old worn-out stories.

Aspiring socialite Buffy Barnswallow is already well regarded in high society, despite being a hockey fan.

It's getting so there is too much red tape attached to Christmas. ❞

> The fellow who leaves a twenty-five-cent tip for lunch always asks the waiter for more crackers.

Being busy is a good thing as we get older, but some days 'just being' is good enough.

Bon vivant bachelor Renaldo Breeze hates to be late, especially when he's meeting temptation.

Veteran newsman Slats Bombauer is teaching his protégé how to investigate a free meal.

Darla Chiffon says, 'Being frugal isn't a bad quality in a husband, as long as he doesn't let his mother cut his hair.'

Forgiveness may be a virtue, but for real satisfaction you can't beat revenge.

Grandpa Bud Babbler

An ex-military man and ultraconservative war veteran, Grandpa Bud would rather go back to jungle warfare than change his mind about anything. A Civil War expert, he used to enjoy researching the Babbler family history until he discovered he is directly related to two Democrats.

A tough old bird, Grandpa Bud's daily health regimen includes eight ounces of whiskey, three cigars, and no salesmen. He blames liberals for everything from traffic jams to tooth decay, and he doubts that there is any benefit in giving Congress the benefit of the doubt.

A terrible driver, he once mowed down his neighbor's hedge while trying to park in his own driveway. Looking at the damage, Grandpa Bud said, "There are too many bushes around here anyway."

> 'Looking at today's politicians, it's easy to see why we've quit building monuments,' says Grandpa Bud Babbler.

Grandpa Bud Babbler has regained his balance five days after taking his grandson on a carnival ride.

Grandpa Bud Babbler says the only time anybody pays attention to the will of the people nowadays is after a funeral.

Grandpa Bud Babbler still sprays a little through his new teeth, but he's furnishing towels.

Grandpa Bud Babbler is in a hurry to have more fun. 'I figure it won't be too long before I'm staring at an aquarium and wondering what teams are playing,' he says.

Grandpa Bud Babbler and his socks have both reached a ripe old age.

“It profits a man or woman nothing if they gain the whole world but have a lousy divorce lawyer.

No one deserves a comfortable place to rest more than a faithful old dog.

Aside from sneezing while eating a carrot, the most annoying thing is a car noise that can't be found.

It's pretty tough to think and hate at the same time.

Jake Clover says the best way to remember your childhood is to tell yourself it wasn't your fault.”

" Shaking hands with the devil isn't nearly as convenient once the election is over.

If the truth be told, everybody's a little bit of a liar.

Ernestine Grizzle has quite a temper. Yesterday she flew off the handle when her new broom broke.

Darla Chiffon could be a poet, but she hates to dress that badly.

One good thing about becoming a hermit is that you don't have any dry-cleaning bills.

You know you've been married a long time when you apologize for something without even getting caught. "

Arlo Berry

An assistant to an assistant bookkeeper, Arlo is so meek that he once bought three dozen hula hoops from a telemarketer. A beleaguered husband, Arlo is dominated by his overbearing wife, whom he refers to as Management. "Management has some powerful mojo," says Arlo. "She can give an order to do something, say how she wants it done, and then remind me to do it right now all in the same sentence."

Arlo, who is always a bit lost, once discovered the road to oblivion while following a road map. A constant worrier, Arlo is such a hypochondriac that he's sure he has glaucoma in his glass eye.

He loves to go to the movies, where he can hide in the dark.

" Arlo Berry called a pest control company at ten o'clock last night to get rid of his dinner guests.

Arlo Berry, who spent two hours yesterday hunched under his desk while talking to someone in India about a computer problem, has been declared legally insane.

Arlo Berry tried to argue with his wife last night, and after fifteen years she remains undefeated.

As a New Year's resolution, Arlo Berry is making extensive plans to be more spontaneous.

Arlo Berry has a new part-time job selling Girl Scout cookies for his daughter.

Arlo Berry stupefied a store clerk today by asking to borrow a phone book. "

❝ While looking for a screwdriver where his wife said she left it, Jake Clover found twelve chocolate wrappers, six hair clips, three double-A batteries, a nail file, a broken pencil, and a pair of pliers.

Here is another tragedy of modern pop culture: the tattooed lady in the circus is obsolete and out of work.

Burning an old tire in the fireplace will almost kill the smell of liver and onions.

Judge Winslow 'TAC' Hammer achieved a personal best today when he handed down sixteen divorce decrees in a mass ceremony.

The only time some people get culture is when they buy yogurt.

Brother Bob Babbler just learned that walking the dog does not count as helping out around the house. ❞

" After six doctor consultations, Dudley Clover has given up trying to wipe the silly grin off his face.

The emperor's new clothes are what all the Washington politicians are wearing this year.

Renaldo Breeze says he was offended when a woman told him he was a terrible flirt. 'I always thought I was pretty good at it,' says Renaldo.

It's downright depressing how some people are always in a good mood.

Some people inherit more money than sense, but not for long.

Two things you can always count on are a faithful dog and a sworn enemy. "

Ernestine Grizzle

A lean and mean school librarian, Ernestine is the crankiest person in Withering Heights. Ernestine hasn't smiled since students glued her card catalog together in 1975, the same year she permanently sprayed her hair in place. A woman of few words – and none of them pleasant – Ernestine believes the best conversations are over quicker than a Las Vegas wedding.

Nicknamed the Hatchet by her students, Ernestine is given a wide berth by even her school colleagues. Ernestine is banned from Withering Heights Botanical Gardens because her mere presence makes flowers wilt.

❝ The only agreeable thing about Ernestine Grizzle is that she can wear beige.

Ernestine Grizzle was feeling so mean yesterday that two viruses passed her by without hesitation.

Ernestine Grizzle has a new hair color, but it still doesn't cover up her mean streak.

Ernestine Grizzle is thinking about retirement, but that doesn't mean she is ready to smile.

Ernestine Grizzle just hired a professional kickboxer to help collect library fines.

Ernestine Grizzle looks two inches taller in her new army boots. ❞

❝ 'I used to dread going to weddings until I started going to funerals,' says Jake Clover.

If it wasn't for their spouses jabbing them in the ribs, some people would never know when to be quiet.

Roxanne Clover's niece has tattoos in all the new spring colors.

A fellow needs to learn early that women consider marriage and hairdos to be serious business.

Theater owner Frosty LaRue is doing just fine. He just bought a new sports car with yesterday's popcorn receipts.

Other than an unemployed relative, nothing settles in as quickly and easily as a bad habit. ❞

> Not even the FBI has ever come up with a lie detector that works better than a good sharp wife.

After weeks of heated debate, the Full Swanky Women's Club of Withering Heights has voted to make tiaras optional at the debutante ball.

Two things that better go right are surgery and a daughter's wedding.

Jake Clover says his wife is looking for a new house with room service.

Nobody has ever stopped a car by stomping the floor on the passenger side, but parents keep trying.

There is a lot more to holding onto a wife than just putting your arms around her.

A Few More Thoughts from the Bard

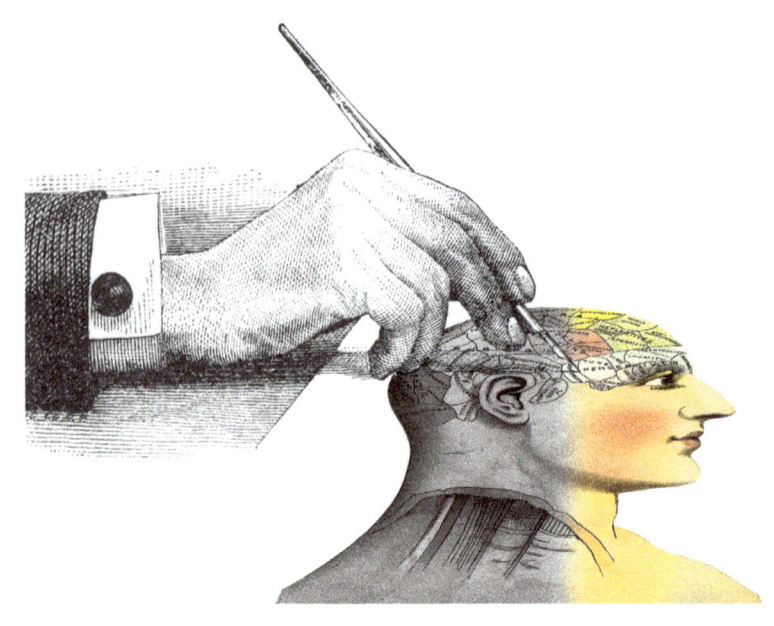

❝ Bea Babbler is looking forward to an early winter after this fall's hot flashes.

Every family has somebody who puts things where you can't find them.

Banker Carlyle Puffington approved a car loan for his mother today after an exhaustive three-month credit check.

Jake Clover doesn't worry about the past. 'My biggest regret is not learning the real words to "Louie, Louie,"' says Jake.

Women are plenty nimble. They can greet one another with a hug and a kiss and somehow still watch their own backs. ❞

❝ J. Wadsworth Fifeington has failed at everything except being an heir and playing croquet.

Nobody we owe money to ever moves out of town.

The circus contortionist known as the Human Pretzel is in Florida for the winter, where he's giving seminars on how to get untangled and pull yourself out of an airplane bathroom.

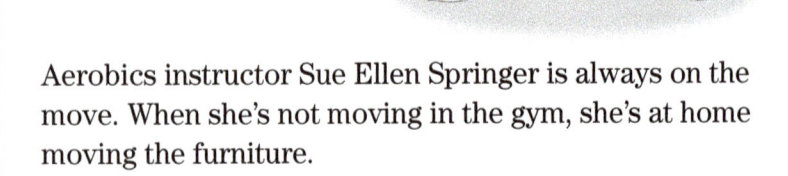

Aerobics instructor Sue Ellen Springer is always on the move. When she's not moving in the gym, she's at home moving the furniture.

One great thing about dogs is that they recognize us for who we are instead of what we are. ❞

❝ What we don't know won't hurt us nearly as much as what we won't admit.

Amateur actress Hilda Bunswaggle opened a new show last night with a song in her heart. Unfortunately, it escaped and reached her voice.

Women keep thinking they'll find a man who likes to sit and talk about feelings all at the same time.

Jake Clover's nephew quit his career as a brain surgeon to become a plumber. He told Jake he wants to make more money.

A summer house is a perfect place to store childhood memories. ❞

❝ There are good reasons for not eating hot dogs, but not good enough reasons.

Philosophical ladies' man Renaldo Breeze says, 'A good woman is like a good book – endlessly fascinating and worth all the attention that's required.'

It's best to avoid hitting a skunk with your car – especially if he's your boss.

Politics has always been a dirty business, but these days you couldn't wash it with a fire hose.

Grandpa Bud Babbler remembers when half a jug would kill any virus known to medical science.

There is no good way to sleep on a hard decision. ❞

❝ The worst advice you can give most people is, 'You should be a singer.'

Jake Clover says the best way to give up drinking is to switch to light beer.

We see way too many politicians who have unlimited limitations.

A fellow who is counting on finding an old-fashioned girl better have a backup plan.

Never take an ugly rumor monger at face value.

There is not much life in a living wage these days. **❞**

❝ In keeping with the latest wedding custom, Bartley Twittle and his fiancée just exchanged engagement nose rings.

A so-so amateur portrait photographer could make a fortune working at a driver's license branch.

Between cell phones and all the varieties of social media, it is now almost impossible to enjoy being unavailable.

We would vote for anybody who could negotiate lasting peace at the dinner table.

Grandpa Bud Babbler just got back from his high school reunion, where he won the prize for having the oldest teeth.

The good-bye that is hardest to accept is the one that goes unsaid. ❞

" Jake Clover says his wife always comes looking for him just when his nap is getting interesting.

It's best not to overdo it when exercising – especially with your opinions.

Of all the savage and merciless creatures on earth, one of the worst is a long-winded bore.

It should be a crime to burn the flag, and there ought to be equal punishment for the way most celebrities sing the national anthem at ballgames.

There is no better use of intellect than to fondly remember a friend.

Teenagers and their parents still have one thing in common: they all want to look twenty-five. **"**

❝ Dudley Clover is so dumb he called a spin doctor to fix his clothes dryer.

An angry spouse won't listen to any excuse, including the truth.

The problem with most politicians is they have nothing to say, and they won't stop saying it.

What it takes for most people to lose weight is the imminent threat of a high school reunion.

Judge Winslow 'TAC' Hammer says, 'Give a criminal enough rope, and he'll tie up the court system.'

What we really need is a health-care bill that cures the nastiness of Congress. ❞

" There are days when the unconditional love of a dog really comes in handy.

How does anyone ever become an experienced lion tamer?

We find out about hidden costs every time we think we're getting something for nothing.

There is nothing like a frown on the face of an enemy to brighten your day.

A lot of people with deep pockets still lead shallow lives.

Speaking of cover-ups, we could use fewer in Washington and more on the beach. "

73

❝ An optimist is someone who believes he is as good as his dog's opinion of him.

Anyone who gets rich quickly will soon find out what his friends are worth.

If being ignorant prevented arguments, there would be a lot more peace and quiet everywhere.

Time is relentless. We just found out that the Age of Aquarius is pushing fifty.

J. Wadsworth Fifeington has that sour, sucking-on-a-lemon face of a lifelong snob.

Everybody is in favor of law enforcement until they get a speeding ticket. ❞

> You never know what free advice will cost you until you act on it.

Integrity and respect can never be acquired with easy down payments.

Some people think it's easier to be against something than to try to understand it.

The best way to give some kids an education is to turn them loose without one.

Nothing changes a fellow's outlook quicker than a kiss from a girl who isn't related to him.

'The first people I'm going after in hell are the ones who hang up after three rings,' says Grandpa Bud Babbler.

❝ Society columnist Pooh Gauzy McFaddish reports that the Full Swanky Women's Club is holding a contest to see whose mother can inspire the most guilt.

We soon get sick of listening to someone who only speaks ill of others.

Good friends, good times, and good dogs make great memories.

Some people never get as far as thinking once, much less twice.

Arlo Berry's 1968 lime-green microbus has finally died of embarrassment.

Jake Clover says getting old is hell. This morning he remembered his wife's birthday but forgot to brush his teeth. ❞

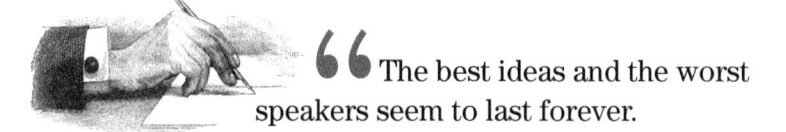

" The best ideas and the worst speakers seem to last forever.

Two things that never seem to get together are having enough time and enough money.

Maxine Mooney is calling in the National Guard to help with this year's zucchini harvest.

Men's Guide to Home Decorating, Rule #1: the furniture in your home looks great where it is until your wife says it will look great someplace else.

Grandpa Bud Babbler is mellowing a bit. He says he's given up bar fighting unless someone really ticks him off.

In this age of mergers, we'd like to see politicians and common sense get together. "

❝ Hedonist Renaldo Breeze says even if somebody managed to live without sin, he'd bet they couldn't do it without regrets.

Social climber Buffy Barnswallow just attended a weeklong finishing school to improve her posturing.

It's good to be taken seriously by everyone but yourself.

Aunt Birdie Babbler is on the far side of sixty, but she can still run down any rumor.

The last man to hear a new idea from a politician died yesterday at age 106.

Any man who doesn't have a wife or a dog better invest in flannel sheets. ❞

It's a Dog's Life

❝ You can't beat a dog's nose for sniffing out food or phonies.

Aside from figuring your taxes, no job is messier all around than washing a dog.

You know you are a dog lover when your dog's bed has a better mattress than yours.

No one appreciates a good nap more than an old dog or a young mother.

It would be a great world if everyone could be as happy as a dog when he's getting fed. ❞

About the Bard

The Bard and the residents of Withering Heights are the creations of Tom Cordell, a retired educational television producer and practicing author. Happily dividing his time between Arizona and Southern California, Tom now avoids work in favor of musing or playing bad golf. He is very good company if you are buying lunch.

About the Illustrator

The characters of Withering Heights also come alive through superb illustrations by Bernie Kapuza. Bernie is a multitalented industrial illustrator, marketing guru, and graphic artist who lives outside of Chicago. The Bard is forever grateful to Bernie for his friendship, impish wit, and visual humor.

CPSIA information can be obtained
at www.ICGtesting.com
Printed in the USA
BVHW092017080519
547776BV00011B/201/P